Modern Curriculum Press
BEGINNING
TO
READ
Series

The Funny Baby

Library of Congress Catalog Card Number: 63-9617
ISBN 0-8136-5016-X (Hardbound)
ISBN 0-8136-5516-1 (Paperback)

3   4   5   6   7   8   9   10   88   87

The Funny Baby

Margaret Hillert

illustrated by Hertha Depper

MODERN CURRICULUM PRESS
Cleveland • Toronto

6

Oh, look.

Here is something.

One little one.

Two little ones.

Three little ones.

And a big one.

Where is the mother?

Can you find the mother?

See here.

Here is the mother.

See mother go.

Look, look.

Mother is here.

Oh, my. Oh, my.

Look in here.

One little one.

Two little ones.

Three little ones.

And—

One big one!

One yellow one.

Two yellow ones.

Three yellow ones.

And—

One is not yellow!

It is not my baby.

Away we go.

We can play.

It is fun to play.

Here I come.

Here I come.

I want to play.

Not you, not you.

You look funny.

Go away.

You can not play.

Oh my, oh my.

I look funny.

I can not play.

I look funny.

I can not help it.

Where can I go?

Away I go.

Away, away, away.

Look up here.

Something is yellow.

Something is red.

Oh, oh, oh.

Look down here.

It is not fun.

Help me. Help me.

Look, look!

See me.

Oh, my!

Away I go!

Look in here.

See me.

It is fun.

Look, look!

Oh, my.

I see something.

Something big.

Oh, oh, oh.

Look down here.

See me.

See me.

See big, big me.

Away we go!

Away, away, away.

Margaret Hillert, author and poet, has written many books for young readers. She is a former first-grade teacher and lives in Birmingham, Michigan.

The Funny Baby

The well-loved tale of the Ugly Duckling, told in charming illustrations and 40 preprimer words.

Word List

7	oh		mother			play
	look		can			fun
	here		you			to
	is		find			
	something	**9**	see		**16**	I
	one		go			come
	little					want
	two	**11**	my			
	three		in		**17**	funny
	and					
	a	**13**	yellow		**19**	help
	big		it			
			not		**21**	up
			baby			red
8	where	**15**	away		**22**	down
	the		we			me

28